LATOYA LAWRENCE

The Pool

This book was professionally typeset on Reedsy.
Find out more at reedsy.com

Contents

Foreword

A native of Queens, New York Latoya Lawrence has been writing since her childhood.

Fourteen other published books by LaToya Lawrence:

The Tantalizing Tales In The City Collection Books 1 and 2-
Forgive Me Father, Secret Admirer

* * *

Inherent: The Birthright, The Session: Murder At Midnight,

Preface

Though surrounded by loved ones and friends Arlette Bardot feels old, lonely, and bored with her life. Filled with nostalgia she longs for the times of long ago when her beauty reigned, and she blossomed in her youth.

Perceiving herself as burnt out and over the hill Arlette seeks rejuvenation in the wrong place.

A mystical remedy to cure her discontentment teaches her a lesson about searching out of her zone for restoration in a tabooed setting.

Arlette learns too late that she should have been grateful for the life she already had instead of chasing behind a fleeting illusion that alluded to her idea of elation.

One

Another Year Older

Arlette Bardot eased from the tub having just showered. She reached for a bath towel then left from the steam-filled room with the support of her 2-wheel walker.

In the milieu of her *Victorian-style* boudoir the woman of old age paused to look at herself in the oval-shaped *Cheval* mirror.

The fine lines and wrinkles that dominated Arlette's once youthful, attractive face had diminished the minuscule appeal that she had left.

During her youth, Arlette remembered how she used to turn heads with her beauty, now all she did was butt heads with *Mother nature* and *Father time* who did not treat her well and do her justice at her age.

The pale-faced light complexioned woman left the dark-cherry wood framed mirror disgusted by her reflection.

She wheeled the silver-grey walker to the queen-size bed then moved her medium, frail body carefully— settling down on the unmade covers of the mattress.

The ivory-colored doors flew open.

Three of Arlette's great grandchildren raced toward the old, undressed woman who sat wrapped in a medium-size bath towel.

"Happy Birthday, grandma!" Wrenlee, Neriah, and Kylian sang out.

The two sisters and brother hopped to the thick, firm mattress of the bed to dotingly wrap their little arms around Arlette.

Surrounded by love and adoration by the young ones—th*e great-grandmother of seven, and grandmother of three*—reciprocated a tight caress with the tight grip of her forearm.

The children had encircled her forming a chain, hugging her with their energetic upper limbs, binding the woman with their affectionate juvenile squeezes.

Arlette patted, then gave Neriah a compress against the back of her hand, conveying both a gesture of love and of appreciation.

"Go get grandma something to put on," Arlette prompted to the six-year-old.

Enthusiastically, the olive-complexion girl with light honey-brown locks twirled in pigtails leaped from the messy covers of the bed across the room to the wardrobe.

Ten-year-old Wrenlee anxiously followed behind to the cream-colored double-doors to the walk-in closet.

In the sanctuary of the minimally lavish, ornate bedroom that embraced the elements of extravagant Victorian-style the place's decor spelled-out modern yet felt the epitome of classic.

A floral-patterned wallpaper partially covered a section of the room. Rich, stately colors that paired beautifully with baroque floral pillows shaded the rest of walls in calm and tranquil textures that added depth to the space.

The design of the modern *Victorian-style* never appeared too trendy or outdated for Arlette's taste the environment suited and complimented her simply fine.

"What about this, grandma!" Neriah said in her baby voice. She had run from the wardrobe to Arlette clutching an item of clothing.

The six-year-old held the garment in the air for Arlette to weigh out for decision. Neriah's anxious brown eyes looking for a response saw her grandmother gaze at the apparel to plumb for something less casual and more elegant for the afternoon outing scheduled today.

Lily, her one and only daughter, and the mother of her own three adult children—*Ellie, Luka, and Remi*—made reservations for lunch at a fancy restaurant Arlette wanted to dress appropriately for the occasion.

Wrenlee in her finesse brought over two other articles of clothing that Arlette favored and chose between.

Two

Engaging Before the Engagement

Arlette gazed her chartreuse-colored eyes at the large gold-colored clock on the *Rockwood terra cotta* shaded walls to the left section of the bedroom from where she stood.

The time read 10:05 am.

Her pocketbook sat against the pillow of the fresh and sophisticated ivory/taupe-colored leather accent chair upholstered in button tufting.

The stylish heirloom piece sat by the three curved bow windows and across from the Zuma white linen upholstered *Wingback* bed.

Dressed immaculately, curled short fluffed white hair done, smelling of crisp fragrant perfume—Arlette grabbed the light powder-blush-colored satchel from the seat of the chair.

The delicate elderly woman of medium size sauntered to the right section of the room toward the fireplace.

On the creamy-velveted diamond button-tufted classic chaise that had a graceful arched back and Golden wood frame that accentuated its silhouette lay her sweater.

She removed the sea-blue colored knitted cardigan from atop the shimmering sage and silver toss pillows.

Arlette then adjusted the *white, silver, pink, gold, cream* shaded south sea pearls of her necklace that matched her lustrous pearl earrings while fastening the row of black buttons to her sweater.

Before the woman headed downstairs to meet Lily, she glanced into the large round mirror hanging on the *downing straw* shaded walls to check her appearance.

Everything looked fabulous to her except for her face and wrinkly hands. Arlette hated how she had aged over the years.

To everyone else she looked simply fine though in their youth and minor aging family did not understand how undesired physical facets brought on by geriatric stages bothered the woman.

Arlette left out from the boudoir of extensive proportion, lofty decorative ceilings, majestically scaled windows, heavy chenille embroidered curtains, ornately patterned carpets and rugs, and intricate structural designs.

She went down the steps to the equally beautified parts of the home she shared with her daughter that flaunted rich and dark hues of *browns, reds, blues,* and *greens.*

The architectural detailing of the entire home was stunning and extremely inviting.

Three

Out And About

Lily Bardot drove her mother to the cemetery to visit a deceased relative's grave before taking the woman of eighty-two years shopping then over to *The White Glove Palate* for a bite to eat.

Along the still, placid turquoise waters skirting the lakeside surrounded by the quintessential elegance of delicate *weeping willows* Arlette walked with the daughter she wholeheartedly cherished.

Amid the charming beauty of drooping branches—*fascinatingly girdled from its canopy hinge*—that grazed the grass and that tinged upon the pavement with their fluttering leaves, the two held hands.

Lily and Arlette admired the scenery and tranquility there shadowing the lanes and pathways of *Sleepy Willow Memorial*

Park.

Down the aisles and throughout the rows of orderly, well-kept headstones the daughter and mother sauntered leisurely in the terrain capturing ravishing sights of deer, rabbits, and birds nesting until they had come upon the gravesite of *Illiana Augustine Bardot*—Arlette's mother and grandmother to Lily.

They both laid down fresh, sweet-smelling bouquets of soft-colored *Anemones* and white/peach *Daffodils*. They spoke words of endearing sentiment calling out to the woman's departed spirit whether she could hear them or not.

After browsing the floors of *Macy's* department store to pick out a choice of outfits and accessories Arlette and Lily ate a big lunch.

By quarter after one in the afternoon, with shopping bags in hand, the women returned home to a celebratory event of decoration, festive food, and a convivial host of ample gatherers.

"Surprise!" Everyone sang out— to then break into an Acapella melody of—**Happy Birthday Dear Arlette**, *H-a-p-p-y B-i-r-t-h-d-a-y To You!"*

The poor woman, absolutely stunned, placed her hand upon her chest as she had almost become shocked to death by the unexpected rip-roar of the crowd.

Arlette overwhelmed by instant hugs and kisses before she made it halfway through the door. Enthralled by colorful streamers, multicolored balloons, people fawning over her, and music that started to play, while abruptly ushered over to the sofa to sit, relax, and enjoy the party secretly prepared for her in her honor.

Four

Wistful

Arlette sat at the windows of her bedroom gazing into the night before she went to bed. She glanced up at the dark-blue sky, the luminescent moon, and the twinkling stars yearning for the days of her youth.

Surrounded by grandchildren who adored her, in laws who respected her, a daughter who catered to her every need, genuine friends who delighted in her company, and an entire family who loved and worshipped the ground that she walked on—Arlette still was not happy.

Instead of focusing on and appreciating the things in life that she did have she pondered about the things that she did not currently have.

The woman had a lovely home, money and wealth, good

health—though her body was not what it once was or as energetic as it used to be she suffered from no illnesses—food to eat and the advantage to travel to any place in the world if she desired.

All those things did not matter to her as much. *They did not faze her.* She would trade it all in a second for the chance to become young again.

Five

Orchard Water Springs

A Month Later

The family had taken notice of what seemed like an acute depression in Arlette. While they did not know the root cause of the problem, or where this obvious discontentment stemmed from, they figured a change of environment may do the woman good.

Everyone had agreed to and had an availability this weekend for a trip over to the Orchard Beach Resort not too far away in their hometown of *Port Springs, New York*. A getaway oasis the entire family could lay back and enjoy without interruption.

Lily's thirty-nine-year-old son and middle child Luka brought his wife Bridget and their two sons Benjamin (eleven) and Theodore (fourteen). Her forty-two-year-old daughter Ellie brought her husband Xavier and their two daughters Danica (twelve) and Finnegan (fifteen). Thirty-six-year-old Remi brought her husband Jett and their three children Wrenlee, Kylian, and Neriah.

Six-year-old Neriah had a brand-new puppy that her parents recently surprised her with two weeks ago coming along on the trip with them to make the brief vacation to the resort complete.

The gorgeous place found at the seaside summer destination of incredible sunsets, clear waters, sandy white beaches, exotic shrubs, granite rocks, sea caves, and steep golden cliffs ministered as a sweet taste of paradise to them all.

The family split up, each venturing out to explore the amenities, atmosphere of seascape, backdrop—and, of course, fun!

"Grandma! Grandma!" Neriah chorused, on her way over to Arlette who laid in a lounge chair in a secluded area on the smooth sands wearing a stylish and versatile sundress that buttoned down the front and tied at the waist.

The woman who sported a trendy pair of sunshades and large floppy brim hat with an elegant bow raised her head at the young one. "What is it dear?"

The olive tone girl with light honey-brown colored hair and dark eyes came close, barefoot, clutching her three-month-old puppy's leash.

"Will you watch Hannah for me? I want to go play in the water."

"Okay, sweetie," Arlette said.

The fair-skinned woman with vivid light greenish-yellow eyes, short colorless hair that had turned white from old age, wrinkles, and discolored patches grabbed a hold of the puppy's leash.

She watched Neriah disappear down the sands of the widespread beach leaving small echoing prints of her footsteps behind. The energetic puppy tugged on its leash eager to follow along with the young child hastily fidgeting to get free.

Cute, adorable little barks and growls hurled from the golden retriever's mouth.

Within a moment, Arlette had dozed off inadvertently allowing Hannah to break free from her grip. The elderly woman awoke to the jolt and to the rattling sound from bells that adorned the puppy's collar.

Hannah took off in the opposite direction of where Neriah had gone.

Arlette tried to move fast as her body allowed with the support of her *all-terrain aluminum beach walker* to catch up to the puppy before she had gotten lost, stolen, or hurt. Hannah ran swiftly around a curved path of zone that appeared private and unfrequented off the coast of the beach.

Bushes, trees, grass, flowers, and weeds dominated this sequestered-looking place that had a pond in its center. Nearby a sign read *No Trespassing*. But it was already too late. Before Arlette could do anything, Hannah had blindly lunged into the standing waters of the pond.

The eighty-two-year-old grandmother covered her eyes in devastation. The dive into the pool had left a fleeting heart-wrenching rippling upon the surface of the water.

How was she going to explain to six-year-old Neriah that her new best friend and beloved pet had drowned on account of her neglect? Arlette felt completely responsible.

Just as the dejected woman went to turn to leave the area she heard bubbling, gurgling, plopping, splashing, swooshing sounds that made her turn back around. Arlette did not believe her eyes. She believed that she had hallucinated when she saw a golden retriever half the size of Hannah appear from the waters of the pond.

Soaked, and shivering, the infant pup that looked just born no longer had its bell-collar or leash attached. Hannah's neck, now too tiny for the collar, had slid right on through the loop of the neckband.

Inconceivably and miraculously the puppy had come back younger.

Arlette had thought she had a problem before now how was she going to explain or even convince Neriah that this puppy was Hannah—the same three-month-old puppy her parents had brought to her from the animal shelter two weeks ago?

Six

What Happened To Hannah?

Neriah cried and cried for Hannah. There was no way Arlette could pull off passing this updated version of Hannah off to the six-year-old child. Maybe if Neriah was younger and/or the gullible type it would have worked. For her age she was too keen and too mentally equip to become fooled within fables or the adolescent fantasies of imagination.

Yet strange and impossible as it may have seemed the pup genuinely was Hannah. *How?* Arlette had no idea. *A mystery beyond her ability to answer, but an enigma to eventually become reckoned with.*

Either way there still would have been explaining for her to do with Remi and Jett.

So, she had to go along with how things appeared though what appeared as reality was not the truth. Arlette fabricated a story about Hannah running away after she escaped from her grip. And that the smaller pup was a replacement.

But how did she find a replacement at the resort in such a short span of time? *Luck, I guess— would have to account for her excuse*, she ruminated. *It is what she would say when the question inevitably came up.*

After time passed, Neriah had gotten over the loss of the golden retriever that she thought she lost. She accepted the duplicate that started to remind and take the place of the irreplaceable Hannah.

Seven

Thoughts In The Summer Breeze

Fifteen-year-old Finnegan walked into the outdoor space of the veranda. The light wood architectures trimmed in white matching the deck with classic stonework and wide, extending columns made for an elegant flare of cozy appeal and comfortable seating.

Arlette shared glasses of sweet tea in the *Port Springs* summer afternoon while she crocheted on the porch swing in the setting of their beautiful upstate New York neighborhood.

"How are you feeling, grandma?" Finnegan—*who the family called Finley in short for her birthname*—asked.

The old woman smiled, sparingly. "I'm okay, child."

Finley wrapped her protective arms around the shoulders of

her grandmother momentarily interrupting the handwork of her needlecraft. The tall, light complexioned teen with medium brown thick flowing hair, and a contagious smile, bestowed to the woman a loving squeeze then sat down beside her to drink tea and talk.

"Are you sure? You have not been yourself lately. You seem distant like you are shutting yourself farther and farther away from us," Finnegan said, concerned.

Arlette stop crocheting for a minute or two to elaborate on the girl's words.

"You know, sweetheart. Maybe when you get my age you will understand. Then again, life may be different for you when you get to be at my age. Sometimes I sit to myself thinking about the past the good times I used to have and how my life is just over now."

"Grandma. Your life is not over. You have us. We have wonderful times with you. Don't you enjoy times spent with us?"

"Of course, I do sugar. But you all are young. You all have your own lives. You have your whole life in front of you. All I get to do nowadays is continue to grow old. Even when I do find enjoyment in certain things, I cannot delight in them the way I would like to—the way I did a time ago. I just can't. Look at me, I am not even as beautiful anymore. I'm old, ugly, and useless."

Ellie happened to have overheard. She had stood by the

screen door listening to her daughter bond with her great-grandmother. Offended by Arlette's words, Ellie appeared from inside the house to the deck of the veranda.

"Grandmother," the medium height woman with brown hair and blond streaks said. "How could you say such a thing? You are the matriarch of this family. You have always been the glue that held this family together. You are not ugly or useless. That is all in your head. You are beautiful inside and out. We would be a mess without you. You are our inspiration we all have looked up to you for so many years and now you are going to disappoint us by putting yourself down and giving up on your life?"

"Grandma just needs something new to do," Finley told her mother. "She has done nearly everything she is just bored."

"Perhaps," Ellie said.

Arlette gave her grand and great-granddaughter a smile an uttered, "There is nothing more left for me to do."

"You are just going through a phase. It is normal. But I do not want to hear any more negative talk from you. It's not good for your well-being," Ellie emphasized.

"Yes, ma'am!" Arlette uttered, putting on a voice of enthusiasm.

Ellie knew the woman well enough to know a forced tone she just hoped Arlette soon snapped out of the funk she was in.

Whatever it was that mentally or emotionally ailed the woman inside did not cause the family serious alarm because Arlette constantly kept up her hygiene, she kept a pleasant attitude toward everyone, she ate properly, and she socialized with her elderly group of friends. She did not neglect herself in any way she just moped here and there projecting misery in her demeanor.

Eight

Sea Change

Two days later, Arlette awoke to an early start. She called a taxi not letting anyone know where she headed. It was her secret. *An idea Arlette had mulled over she finally decided to conduct to satisfy her inquiring mind for the last time.*

The eighty-two-year-old woman paid the cabdriver then strolled the seaside of Orchard Beach in Orchard Water Springs without the use of a walker. She had left the mobility device at home hoping she would not come to need it later.

Arlette went to the secluded area of beach-land where she last occupied to sneak around to the restricted location off limits to the public.

A short distance away from the sandy shores the woman approached the forbidden pond surrounded by weeds, flowers, bushes, green grass, and bountiful trees. Arlette boldly undressed, stripping every inch of clothing from her wrinkly, sagging, frail, discolored body.

She braced herself with each step she took toward the water, not knowing what to expect, while expecting the water of the pond to feel cold.

Arlette baptized her body in the loch she assumed shallow. She surprisingly sunk in deep the moment she entered the pond. The water swallowed her up enveloping her in its pool of clear mystical juice.

Helplessly buried underneath the thick, liquid moisture for the three minutes that felt abnormally long Arlette appeared from the waters thirty-years younger. Soaked, and shivering, the woman in the fifty-two-year-old body rushed to put on the clothes she had left lying on the mass of greenery.

Nine

Going For Mint Condition?

The Next Day

Arlette managed to return home yesterday afternoon without the detection of family members. When she refused to leave from her bedroom for dinner, she made up the excuse of feeling ill.

The mother of one, and grandmother of ten altogether between grands and great grands, did not know how long she could evade the people in the household. If she kept avoiding her relatives for long, they would get suspicious drawing unwanted attention toward herself.

Ellie and Luka did not live there at the home only Lily did. However, they often came to visit.

Remi and her husband Jett lived in their own condominium while their children stayed over with Lily and Arlette when they worked or opted out of hiring a regular babysitter to watch the kids.

Arlette did not want to live concealed she wanted to show and thrive in her upgraded body but how would she explain the sudden radical change in appearance? Plastic surgery the slickster conveyed to a stunned group of family and friends once she had produced a plausible reason to pass off as truth.

The formally white mane that had now turn brown she claimed was a dye-job.

Lily and her adult children were not pleased with what they knew as Arlette's complete reconstructive make-over. The idea of going through such a dangerous cosmetic procedure at her age without consulting any of them just did not sit well or receive their instant approval.

Though the mother and grandmother looked exceptional—*contributing to a noticeably assured outlook and self-image*—they preferred her in the natural growing old gracefully.

Ten

The Fountain Of Youth

The novelty had begun to wear off for Arlette. The fifty-two-year-old body she wore no longer suited or satisfied her. The eighty-two-year-old who defied the natural laws of order wanted the ultimate. She thrived for perfection—a face and body far from one in their fifties, or forties.

This anomalous transformation met a need, yet it did not fulfill a purpose, not to the extent of what she strove to obtain.

Arlette returned to the pond to bathe in its magic a second time. She dived into the peculiar waters to materialize in the likeness of a woman in her early twenties. Arlette appeared fit, supple, and gorgeous. She could not believe her eyes when she saw her reflection in the mirror.

She had to see for herself what provoked the whistles, smiles, eye winks, flirts, and stares from men who inhabited the beach resort of *Orchard Water Springs* on her way from the restricted area she dared to infringe upon. Arlette had not received attention of this size in decades.

Everywhere she went she turned and spun heads.

Eleven

Delectable Queen On The Scene

Expert at portraying an extremely younger person in comparison to her actual age, Arlette fell into the effortless role of reminiscence. It all had come back from the yesteryears to replay and playback during this period of the present.

Arlette strutted in a spaghetti-strap bathing suit. Her long thick straight brown locks pinned abundantly in a bun. Three silky moist strands clung against her oval-shaped face. A chic pair of sunglasses sat attractively at the bridge of her pert-shaped nose covering her dazzling emerald-green eyes.

The red tinted shades that partly concealed the woman's long thick brows highlighted the flawlessness of her cream-colored complexion and luscious thick, red-painted lips.

An impeccably striking vision of splendor Arlette showed to

everyone.

Twelve

The Cost Of Her Fulfillment

After hours basking in the glow of admiration the day had ended. Beachgoers collected their items and accessories from the warm, gritty white sands of *Orchard Water Springs Beach and Resort.*

People gathered to leave, vehicles pulled off, the public seemed to have vanished within brief moments of time.

All alone and no longer the center of attention. Arlette's audience consisted of the day turning into night, the deep pinkish-blue-white skies, the gentle current of the ocean, the tides reflecting their waves in the moonlight, and the swaying of trees blowing amid the coolness that intertwined the temperate of breeze.

Clasping a pair of sandals between her agile fingers barefoot in the sand Arlette grabbed her mobile phone from the inside pocket of her purse and called a taxi.

Lily had worried about her mom throughout the day. She had left and been gone for hours. *Where was she? Why had she not phoned? Why did she not return her calls?* Dinner stewed over the stove. Lily kept the food warm in case Arlette had walked in late. The nervous woman in her sixties put the grandchildren to bed. They had already eaten.

A key turned in the keyhole. Lily heard the door to the side entrance of the house unlock.

"Finally, she's home," the woman said to herself, relieved. Lily removed the kitchen apron from around the back of her neck and waistline then hung the garment upon a hook on the wall.

"Whew! What a day I have had, uttered a voice coming from the inside steps by the side door. "All I want to do is have a nice bubble bath then hit the sack."

"Who are you?" Lily said.

The woman with pale skin whose fringed light-brown bangs hung evenly above her hazel/green eyes demanded to know how this unfamiliar young lady had gotten a key to walk into her home the way she did.

"What do you mean who am I?" Spoke the woman who appeared to look about twenty years of age. "I am your mother."

Unamused and feeling disregarded, Lily became belligerent.

"Okay, I am going to ask you one more time—who the hell are you and how did you get a key to my house?!"

"Lily?" The old woman said. "Calm down."

"And how do you know my name!"

Then it dawned on Arlette. She had come in preoccupied, distracted, and inattentive of her surroundings. Lost in thought, and unheeding, she had fleetingly forgotten how she currently differed from the woman who left home earlier during the day.

She took for granted that Lily would have been up in her bedroom by now. If she had it would have bought her a proportion of time. At least she could have slept upon the incident and tried to produce something believably outlandish in the morning if possible.

Before Arlette could get out another word Lily furiously snatched the house keys from this stranger's hands then thrusted her back out the side door.

"These are my mother's keys! How did you get them?! Where is my mother? I swear nothing better had happened to her! I am calling the police right now, young lady!"

Arlette stepped away from the side of the home. In sandals, a dungaree skirt, and a thin-strap bathing suit as a top, the old woman with a young body disappeared down the street to call another taxi—this time to drop her off at a hotel for the evening.

While on her mobile phone the woman bearing a semblance unrecognizable to family and friends had undergone an unexplainable modification that landed her in a bind. In her quest for youth and the chance to revisit her prime Arlette had not thought about the consequences. She leaped ahead imprudently and injudiciously, nonetheless, the woman still was in a place of temporary gratification. Arlette elated, and on cloud nine, had gotten what she wanted, and it had come with a heavy price.

Thirteen

Life From Herein

A week had passed. Arlette sat on a park bench lonely and desolate, but strikingly gorgeous and extremely youthful. The thing she yearned for the most was the only thing in the world that she had left.

Her income had run out. Access to her bank account had come to a halt since Lily reported her mother missing. When Arlette went to use her debit card at the *ATM* to withdraw retirement funds paid to her from *Social Security* the automated teller machine declined the transaction.

Unable to confront a bank-teller and withdraw money in person at the bank or prove her identity to anyone as Arlette's current altered appearance did not match the face of the eighty-two-year-old woman captured in the photo of her New York state ID.

Arlette saw the missing posters of her former self across from where she sat plastered on tree-barks and in other places around town. The age defying woman remembered seeing and approaching her eldest great-grandson Theodore on the street six days ago. The fourteen-year-old boy became hostile toward her when she tried to tell him she was his great-grandmother who had undergone another extensive reconstructive procedure.

"You are not my great-grandmother," Theodore had told her. "You are sick. You must be the same lady my aunt said came into her house with her mother's keys telling her that you were her mother. Who are you? Why are you saying you are my great-grandmother when you know you are not? You are stupid!"

Arlette had felt bad. One of her own beloved kin rejected her not knowing or believing who she claimed to be. The instance was devastating and disheartening for the woman who had become nonexistent.

Certain men on the street had an extreme attraction to Arlette and a sum of them would have taken her in whether to use her or to develop a relationship but this is not what Arlette wanted. These people did not know or care about her.

She had no friends to go to because no one knew who she was and starting a new life over to meet new people or career goals seemed impossible without proof of identification. Aside from a photo ID there was no birth certificate, social security card or any other type of credentials to verify and confirm her place in society.

The only thing that may have convinced people at least of her family ancestry was through DNA. *Then maybe Lily would accept her.* It was a long shot because she would never believe Arlette was her mother.

Lily would come to accept she was related to them somehow through blood tests, but as a relative she had never met, or heard of, where or who in the family could Arlette say that she birthed to and had come from? No one of their relatives distant or near could vouch for her as their own.

Arlette did presently look identical to pictures of herself when she entered her twenties yet that only served as a coincidental factor in the eyes of certain others. It did not mean she really was another version of Arlette.

What did strike Lily and her nephew oddly when they confronted one another after both having a run in with this Arlette impersonator is that she did have the old woman's voice. They had concluded whoever the young lady was she just faked Arlette's vocal tones.

Lily and Theodore did not know her motives, but they talked to the police and the authorities were currently out looking to investigate by searching for and bringing this woman in for questioning in the disappearance and ridiculous impersonation of Arlette Bardot.

Fourteen

A Sad Story

Another three weeks had passed, and Arlette was homeless. In the summer season she did not suffer as she would have if it were winter. The woman did not necessarily have to become homeless as she could have gone to a shelter and eventually found the legal means to create a new identity.

However, though she looked one way on the outside Arlette felt an entirely separate way on the inside. Physically she had her youth but mentally and biologically she was the same elderly individual with ineffaceable experiences and ineradicable time left here on earth.

The indelible chapters of Arlette's past and future life could not go dismissed nor avoided. The twenty-year-old body she walked around in held the same eighty-two-year-old woman whose years did not come extended when she traded her outward features in that pond.

Arlette deeply regretted her mistake. She wished that she never had met the mystery that horribly beguiled and enchanted her in the restricted waters apart from the shores of Orchard Beach. The area was off limits for a reason and now she knew why.

The woman terribly missed what she once had. The beautiful love and life with family that she did not appreciate enough. Arlette would give anything to look in the mirror and see that old wrinkly woman with age spots and fine lines again.

She thought regaining her youth would bring the joy and vibrancy back into her life. Now in hindsight she saw that she had already had a happiness and zest cascading within her life—a treasure that did not come around often. A precious fortune she did not know the value of and one that she foolishly gave away for nothing.

Arlette sobbed. She was homesick and crushed knowing she could never return home to the ones she loved—and who loved—and had forever lost her.

Fifteen

The Pond

Arlette stood naked and smelly from not bathing in a while. Surrounded by the wild weeds, thick bushes, array of flowers, sprouting grass, and luxuriant trees in front of the forbidden pool of ominous fate she closed her eyes to make a heartfelt wish.

She begged for the opportunity to turn back into the likeness of her old self, and if not, then she begged for death to consume upon her this very day.

On the verge of taking one last leap into the pond to undo or end this unfavorable circumstance Arlette braced herself before daring to delve into the unknown once again.

A huge splash came from the plunge into the water. Then for a moment there was silence.

Three to four minutes later—*which felt more like ten minutes,* a small body the size of a two-year-old appeared from the pool.

The toddler eerily and unearthly floated from the pond to crawl onto the grass. Unable to completely walk and talk without babbling, cooing, and falling from an unsteady gait Arlette had materialized from the pond this third time as a baby.

Trapped inside the body of a defenseless child Arlette panicked as her attempt at redemption had punished her further. This occurrence was far from anything that could have ever crossed Arlette's mind.

The woman had to accept the recondite episode that she could do nothing about.

This paranormal pool bestowed a curse to result into an inconvenient blessing for Arlette. Now that she was a child, someone was sure to scoop her up into their arms to clothe, feed, bathe, and provide shelter.

About the Author

Hello!

I am a writer who does not limit herself to one specific genre. I write by what naturally inspires me at any given time as I am naturally versatile- whether it be self-help, devotional, non fiction or fiction novels of suspense.

One thing I have observed through my writing, and with life in general- as certain others have I am sure, is that people will view things and/or judge within their own perception- viewing through their own personal lenses.

What they may interpret or misinterpret may not at all correspond or have anything to do with what I or another may be expressing, divulging, or projecting.

All of us writers do not use ourselves as examples, yet we may share what we have seen or encountered through others first-hand while also adding to our own experience as a confirmation to what we know is fact or a possibility.

As writers and as human beings, we will always receive some form of criticism, praise, or misjudgment.

It is all up to the individual on how they accept, handle, or ignore what others throw out.

I personally am a very strong, resilient, determined person who cannot be swayed by the judgment or opinions of others.

When we write and live life, we are not always going to please others- and I do not seek nor have I ever sought validation or approval from anyone.

I have God-given talents just like a lot of us do, and writing is something I have loved to do since my childhood and is my passion.

If anyone chooses to learn or feel enlightened or inspired by my writings, then so be it. If not, so be it.

I do not write to please or to disturb anyone I write because it is one of my callings as I am extremely creative.

There is nothing wrong with sharing and exchanging ideas.

I also feel that as a writer one should never let anyone discour-
aged them in their ventures or visions.

Always stand up for yourself and what you believe in and if
others misunderstand you or persecute you for any reason that
is their problem not ours.

Some people in life will relate to others in some form or fashion
and some will not- and that is a good thing.

Most of the time their words and/or actions are a reflection of
themselves and not of us.

We as individuals all cannot be the same. If so, life would be
dull and boring.

Be happy, be healthy, and publish the beauty of your diversity
of talent until your heart is content!

We all have something wonderful to contribute to the world. -
Latoya Lawrence

Also by LaToya Lawrence

A natural born writer from childhood to adulthood.

Inherent
The Bledsoe Clan- Occult Power in The Bloodline

From Caul births to the calling of the Orishas into the pathways of the Yoruba religion to the mystical powers that inhabit the universe.

Festivity, food, fashion, creative celebratory culture. Living a lifestyle aligned to their nature.

Unorthodox, unapologetic, and unafraid.

Wishing well are wishes that come true as they do for Emery Bledsoe. In her rich culture and heritage, she learned early what she was able to do.

The enigma to attract what she wanted had uncannily come as an advantage throughout her unusual, extraordinary life.

In what she has taken for a natural stroke of luck in her transcendent genealogy of hidden bloodline turns into something far more eldritch and unnerving than she ever thought imaginable once she receives a bestowal handed down to her in the form of a stunning vase.

A family heirloom presented as a beautiful gift turns into an odious curse that Emery is unable to break away from.

In the escape of her world where all the doors have shut closed will she find the key to forever set her free?

The Bakery Boutique: Desserts To Die For

Jordanna's customers are dropping like flies when they buy and consume the decadent array of incomparable and matchless handmade pastries of her family-owned bakehouse that are literally a cut above the rest in comparison to her competitors.

Is there something speculative in the recipe? Could it be the unethical managing of an employee? Could there be a contamination somewhere in the ingredients of specific items ordered and delivered to the shop? Or is the sudden fatality of consumers who patronize Irresistible Bites Bakehouse just victims of their own demise or unfortunate circumstance?

Detective Grayson Waylon would sure like to know the answer as he is the lead investigator boggled by the mystery behind a string of unsolved deaths undetectable by medical examiners conducting autopsies on the bodies that start to build up.

In a case of unknown causes of death tied to a common thread there is no evidence to show or to prove Jordanna's bakery as the main source for foul play.

Fatal Beauty: When Love Kills

Do to others as you would have done unto you or do to others what they have done to you? One should ask Delilah, the beauty with a score to settle against those who inhabit her world.

When an incident of disturbance shake-up Delilah's life, she becomes twisted, diving into the arms of men who cannot resist her fire. Ready to burn each one in her passion- things turn deadly.

While Delilah plays a dangerous game of laying traps for those who cannot break free- even when she chooses to let go and cut loose- danger comes to bite back at a cost where murder inevitably will pay.

LaToya Lawrence

Lady

In this fictional California town of Ramona life is kind until a sudden flow of recent events come to threaten the immediate future of a young woman who is resistant to change and not prepared for the misfortune that occurs.

When all goes wrong, and Cora Eckhart's life turns upside down she chooses a path that leads into a world of uncertainty, instability, and risk.

Aware of the imperilment that she faces, Cora has a plan, one that eludes the law and those who are blazing on her trail.

With nothing else left but to fight and to survive, she takes on a double life that takes the lives of others in the survive of her fight.

As Cora unwittingly outsmarts others in her anomaly in crime will her luck eventually run out or will she escape into the new life that she aspires to create?

The Session: Murder At Midnight
Bambi is a trusted therapist who clients put their money and trust in. They share to her their innermost feelings and spill their deep darkest secrets.

Bambi thought she had heard and seen it all until this one unusual client comes in for a session and manages to get inside to pick her brain.

Bambi eventually starts to lose her grip and begins to wonder who the therapist is and who the client is.

In a head game of truth and revelation, will this new client serve as a hard nut to crack- or will Bambi end up the one to crack up enough to kill?

The Backwater Summer Lake Resort: The Forbidden Lake

What is lurking in the clear waters of Lake Cahuilla in upstate White Oaks, New York? It seems when those that dive in for a cool splash or to take a rejuvenating swim, they do not always make it out of the loch alive.

In such a lovely, inviting atmosphere there at the *Backwater Summer Lake Resort* And *Water Park*- where there is luxury lodging at the *Red Brick Villa*, luxury dining at the *Lakeside Hideaway*, luxury coffees and pastries at *Cahuilla Lakeside Café*, luxury entertainment and drinks at the *Swinging Cahuilla Cocktail Lounge*, luxury lake boat rides on the *Brave-Waters Expedition*, local luxury spots of recreation and pastimes to indulge in at *All Things Books Bookstore*, *The Happy Hangout Jazz Club*, *The Reel Zone Movie Theater*, *The Lavender Boutique Department Store* in addition to a host of other places to explore- how could anything of a threatening nature go unresolved or undetected?

Or is what is quietly held by those as superstition kept hidden, and what is held as superstitious dread, considered water under the bridge?

And what is the strange connection between Lake Cahuilla and two young sisters who live in a town of New York nowhere near White Oaks? Why are they drawn to a place they have never been to and had no prior knowledge of before becoming aware of its existence?

Is this all-just coincidence or is there something in the backwaters of their past that they do not remember calling out to them to send them a chilling message that will explain an incident from the past that will also have a positive impact on their future?

Forgive Me Father
Book 1 of 2: Tantalizing Tales In The City

Who is murdering the young students that attend Saint Josephine Margaret Bakhita Preparatory School?

As the bodies mysteriously build up shock and scandal erupt on the grounds of a private parochial school affiliated with the neighboring church and convent that serve and inspire the community.

Is the killer the obvious suspect or the one that everyone least expects committing these awful, brutal crimes?

Will the true killer escape capture? Or will the innocent person pay the penalty for the sins of another? Or could it just be the one suspected at the start the true murderer there right under everybody's nose?

Secret Admirer
Book 2 of 2: Tantalizing Tales In The City

Welcome To the Tantalizing Tales Collection: Toya's Titles of Terror, Treachery, And Suspense Shorties *Volume Two*

In Volume two of this series two separate stories take place—the first a continuation from **Book one** that moves into its own tale of torture.

And the second, a standalone that moves in line with another one of its own quirks and craziness.

Enjoy the out of the ordinary ride!

Tale One:

Secret Admirer

Bryce Brandon has found the love of his life—the only woman for him—but someone else is looking to take this lovely lady's place. Watching and waiting behind the scenes for the opportunity to snatch Bryce up for them self this mysterious individual will stop at nothing to get their hand on the object of their affections, and fervent desire—even if it causes them to kill for it!

Tale Two:

The Dollhouse

Lorna Ferguson is a twelve-year-old loner with a secret. A secret she likes to incorporate into her alone time play. The games in her life become real. The reality of her games become deadly. This young girl does not play when it comes to others or those that cross her, so do not play with this little girl—if you do it may cause you your life!

New York Style Tales Of Suspense: Tantalizing Tales In The City
Three short stories that include thrills in a mixture of fictional towns around New York.

New York Style: Tales of Suspense Tantalizing Excitement in The City! – *Join this two hundred sixty-five-page psychological thrill ride of murder, mystery, suspense, a bit of the supernatural, and fun!*

Tale one: Two Of A Kind

Is Blood thicker than murder?

There is a secret buried deep in the soil of Cherry Hill. In a town of beautiful cities, lakes, and villages where trees grow tall, flowers bloom free, and the neighbors are friendly.

Is there an uncovered truth rising upon the surface? One of cruelness among rebellious youth? Or could it just be a hereditary factor where bloodline goes bad, and murder goes right.

Mysterious murders take place in the lovely upscale town of Cherry Hills throughout Pennington, New York—killings and deaths that shock and bewilder residents in a city where scandalous crimes run sparse. There had not been such incident since the highly publicized murders that took place in early winter of January 1981 on Oakwood St. in the home of Evelyn and Ryan Barker.

Tale two: The Lovers

What is it that is masquerading as ordinary, lurking brazenly on forbidden territory? Is there a price for playing with magic or is magic worth paying the price for?

Deep in the city streets of Manhattan lies a place for those who want to take a gamble at chance.

One may get lucky, or one may lose out.

In any fashion, delving in, one must accept the consequence that what was bought cannot be returned as there is no way to buy back what was once sold.

It is not wise to mess with things that are considered taboo as what is taboo can come back around to mess with you.

A young man consults a voodoo priest and gets more than he bargains for when he takes home a personalized spell-kit, and all goes wrong.

Tale three: Summer Fling

In a world of their own craziness, impulse, and greed, do you really know who the people around you are when they do not even know and cannot trust themselves?

Riding on a rollercoaster they cannot function to get off of—continuously spinning around only to come to nowhere to get them back to their sphere.

Dealing with them is enough to drive one crazy but a little craziness allows one to deal with the drive to survive.

A successful woman takes a setback to bounce back in her career even stronger than ever before— inciting unknown events from the past of those around her to reveal mind-boggling secrets and mysteries that result in a multiple chain of unexpected murders.

Danielle's Diary
In this fictional town of Westbrooke, Staten Island, on Stanton Boulevard fifteen-year-old Danielle struggles with the pain of constant violation. And Kelly, her drug-addicted mother ignores her complaint.

Danielle has no other choice but to suffer the abuse of a drug dealer living within their home.

Kelly's dependency on Bruce, her drug dealing boyfriend, outweighs all other matters that are concerned and with no one to turn to and nowhere to run Danielle endures a life of misery until one day when she is saved by her long lost father, Marcus Glover.

Wellness In Style
Coping, managing, living, and enjoying ways of life on one's own terms suitable to their nature.

Motivation, counsel, and encouragement to self-betterment.

Harmonic Inspirations
Poetic motivation and literary writings of counsel and encouragement through creative self-expression

experience.

God Has The Last Word
Spiritual and Intellectual counsel, and encouragement through creative motivational self-expression from true life

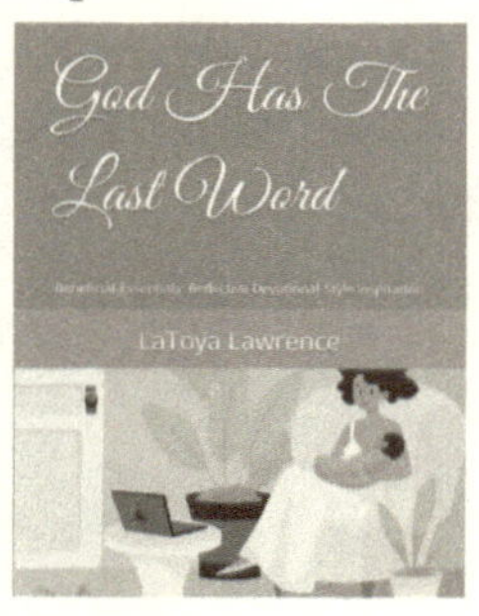

My Cup Overflows

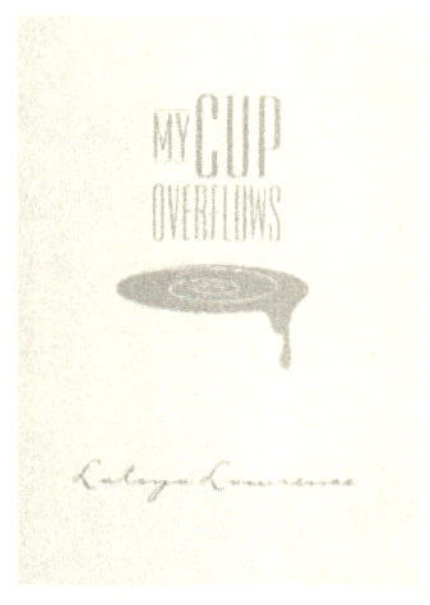

on the rise.

Jaxon.

When Love Kills
In this follow up to Fatal Beauty emotions run high while tempers flare out of control.

From the brutal actions of a woman scorned to the husband and mistress that drove her into rage- a binary fury savagely

Violent repercussions stir the pot of a dish on the menu called revenge that in this quandary is best when served either hot or cold.

Nothing held back, and no one is spared from the deadly wrath of a mother hell-bent on payback for the vicious/malicious attack on her beloved daughter, Delilah

The Whispering Staircase

In the beautiful county of Luxaha on the coast of the Notaro Bay shores above the Tomosa river in the city of Winterly, Virginia sits the luxurious home of the wealthy African American Dorrance family who propitiously struck gold in the oil and gas industry.

Inside the extravagant mansion covered on lush, opulent grounds-filled with amenity and high-end living-lies a dark secret waiting to become unfold.

When Deane Dorrance arrives home one night to find that a seemingly accidental death had taken place on the staircase like the incident on the staircase that had taken place seven years before the woman views the occurrence as an eerie coincidence.

When a police investigation reveals the death on the steps resulted from murder the case becomes open and shut then solved once the killer was learned and later found deceased.

After the case closes and time moves on whispering clues start to speak of a mystery that sinuously hides beneath. Turnabouts behind the connection of the staircase surround to expose a sinister truth of lies betrayal, greed, and shock.

The Demons
Welcome To the Tantalizing Tales Collection: Toya's Titles of Terror, Treachery, And Suspense Shorties *Volume Three—Enjoy the ride!*

Story One:
The Demons

Tricia Newman moves into her new apartment to find out that she is not the only one occupying residence there.

At first, she believes she is just burdened by unwelcome four-legged guests of the rotund kind to find out something more sinister is lurking behind the scenes.

Mice and rats are the least of Tricia's problems when she discovers a host of monstrous creatures running around to horrifyingly wreak havoc and wrestle her into their demonic world.

Story Two:
Oliver The Mute

If anyone knows how to keep a secret it is Oliver Tujari. No one can pry anything out of him his lips stay sealed. Too quiet in his silence everyone wonders why twelve-year-old Oliver will not speak a word.

Is he shy? Does he feel he may say the wrong thing? Or is he just tongue-tied?

While people criticize young Oliver and even inflict violence upon him due to his non-verbal communication—when he finally does open, it is a moment that anyone within his presence will deeply regret.

Story Three:
  Night Chaser

The role of a good Samaritan Indigo Jones decides not to become when someone in need earnestly reaches out to her for help.

This lady of the night saw something that she was not supposed to see.

In her wander throughout town Indigo is not the only one to roam around the street all morning long. The tables take a turn, and this unlucky lady ends up running for her life.

Will she escape what is in the night or will the night take Indigo down for the chase?

Ersha's Eyes
Welcome To the Tantalizing Tales Collection: Toya's Titles of Terror, Treachery, And Suspense Shorties *Volume Four*

In this fourth volume and final installment there are four entertaining tales— in the beginning, find out what happens to the characters from the first story in volume three before the chapters enter and develop into its own addictive chaos.

Afterward, two more tormenting tales to indulge in.

Enjoy the ride!

Story One:
  Ersha's Eyes

Haunted by puzzling, cryptic, tormenting visions Ersha Bigelow becomes a victim of circumstance. Something chillingly hovers over her in the ongoing of her life. Something elusive that Ersha is unable to put a finger on.

Constantly burdened by spooky images, eerie shadows, and enmeshing dreams— thoughts, images, and sensations found within the intangible realms reach out to her in the arena of the tangible.

Precognitive insight that once guarded from mistaken or misguided actions or judgments turn into premonitions that lead her into danger, deception, and darkness.

Story Two:
   The Supplement

Tessa Arley is going bald at the age of twenty-seven. She is too young to lose her hair. Doctors cannot understand or find the root cause for the condition that threatens to ruin her confidence and take a toll on her life.

After all tests and treatments do not produce a diagnosis and solution to the problem Tessa continues to not only lose her hair at a more rapid rate, but she starts to lose hope.

One day while Tessa is visiting her dermatologist, he recommends a clinical trial to assess out a new drug for unexplainable hair loss. Tessa takes the doctor up on his offer as nothing else has worked in the past.

When the study appears to help Tessa giving her the unbelievable results, she never thought possible—could this new experimental drug be the magic formula to her miracle cure or is it all just too good to be true?

And what about the side effects?

Do the advantages outweigh the risks or are the risks worth the consequences?

Story Three:
   Blood Meal

Landon Sanders finds out from a neighbor that screams had come from the unit of his condominium while he spent another one of his days busily at work. He enters his home to the inclination of his grandmother's presence yet there is no sign of her anywhere.

A day or two later, Landon brings a date home and while he is in the bathroom the gushing sounds of alarming screams ring out. Then, like his grandmother, his date disappears.

Is there a connection between the two? Is there something bloody strange going on?

Story Four:
  Sealed Fate

When Harlyn Stone goes to a fortune teller to get her future read the circumstance may unfortunately lead to the end of her future.

The Artist: When Paintings Come To life

Aspen is an artist with a hidden talent one that goes beyond his paintbrush and easel.

While he is successful in his work life as a cartoonist and comic book illustrator loved by both his sister Amiyah and his best friend Xander he suffers immensely in his personal life.

Aspen has no luck with the ladies. Women that he finds interest in have no interest in him.

They paint him out as one who they could not picture themselves with and there is no shortage to them expressing their unkindness and showing him their cruelness. Fed up with the constant mistreat and disrespect from the objects of his affection, Aspen directs all his energy into the skill and beauty of his craft.

When his remarkably stunning works of art become recognized as extraordinary masterpieces women from the past have a sudden change of heart and now cannot help but find Aspen overwhelmingly irresistible.

As the ladies fall at Aspen's feet are they really looking at him through a new set of eyes or are they artfully led by the stroke of a brush?

In this cryptic tale of resentment and revenge—*a hand once dealt becomes the hand that deals out*—the man who the women could not picture themself with is the man who draws their life painting then brings their fatal portraits to life.

Friends

Do lies become the truth within corrupt situations? Or is it that malicious actions and scandalous deeds are justified by those who believe in their own untruths?

Deep in the heart of the small, quiet, picturesque rural and urban towns of upstate New York lie lust, greed, jealousy, deceit, murder, and mystery among those who call themselves friends.

In an environment of this nature, one would surely ask—*who needs enemies when you have friends like these?* These people do more than smile in each other's faces while plotting behind one another's backs.

Bold and shameless facades, suspect behavior, shady dealings, cruel backstabbing—you name it! There is plenty of indecency to go around and no one ever knows who will turn and do what next.

In a place filled with spontaneous attractions, insatiable appetites, selfish desires, changeable minds, and a range of unpredictability there is bound to be a hint of danger lurking around in the air.

The Cafe Lounge
Join Rowan Haynes in his venture to France to start new after he loses the love of his life.

Finding it hard to get over Aurora his sister, Nola Hayes, recommends for him to spend time off from his job to take a vacation to France—*where she lives and is the manager of her own cafe.* A cafe that just further serves as a reminder of Aurora as she once worked at the *Bakery Boutique Irresistible Bites Bakehouse* and *Cafe* back in *Long Island*, the first place they had ever met before dating and coming close to marriage.

On Rowan's vacation from Roslyn, New York—*which Nola hopes will become her brother's permanent location to settle down and make a home there*—he finds himself the spectator in the swindle and entanglements that inhabits the cafe when he starts to work at the cozy, inviting place.

Amid three crooks, a reformed hustler looking for love and to live an honest life, and a nice young lady the victim of mistaken identity and circumstance—*who regularly visit the shop*— a heap of unexpected mix-ups, mishaps, and mischief unravel in front of the eyes of Rowan and Nola where they inevitably get involved to help solve a crime and save the day from a trio of villains wanted by the police for a chain of ongoing heists throughout the cities of France.

On This Day: A Marriage Made In Murder

A marriage made in heaven, or a marriage made in hell

Ask Paisley Cresswell as she has taken one of her vows extremely seriously—*until death we part.*

Paisley does not plan to stay around for bad or for worse or for in times of sickness or prospering health.

Some people get married for love, some people get married for security, some people get married because of pressure from their family, and some people get married for show.

Paisley got married to tie up loose ends. Yet at the end of a plan to cut all ties—*a means to an end becomes a knot not so able to be loosely untied.*

LaToya Lawrence

Paper Dolls

From the suspense thriller "Lady" comes "Paper Dolls" a standalone novel with the late Ingrid Eckhart's daughter undertaking a high-stake in her career after the death of her mother then later running into the unabating Tex Hayes and Rory Holden—the lieutenant and sergeant—who would stop at nothing in their mission to take down her niece—the infamous Cora Eckhart—from the first tale in this elegantly told gritty trilogy saga.

After scouting for talent to conduct a casting call, project manager and ex fashion model turned photographer Irma Eckhart uncovers the start of a deadly mystery she never saw coming.

Models smile for the camera then bliss turns into bloodshed when handpicked aspiring fashion models in search of their dreams land gigs that take them abroad to the exquisite, fascinating countries of Italy, Spain, England, and France.

These fresh-faced young ladies with killer-looks find more than they expect when their counterparts start vanishing at every turn going ignored by their fanatical photography crew whose primary concern is satisfying their high-end clients and meeting the strict deadlines for their projects.

Sierra

Ten-year-old Sierra Matisse is an intelligent, quiet girl who certain other children do not understand and make fun of.

To them she is extremely unique, strange, and hard to figure out. Sierra even incites jealousy and intimidation within these children that cause them all to act out and behave ill towards the young child.

As school children and neighborhood children band together to bully, control, and to ruin Sierra's sense of self-value to make her their easy target—Sierra turns the tables and surprises them with her extraordinary attributes bestowed to her by birth.

Proving that she is the one to be feared, the children all learn a tough lesson in messing with the wrong kid—as it could inevitably cost them their lives.